AWAKENED

The Tom Meadows Series

Jake Victor Guzman

Awakened: The Tom Meadows Series

For information contact:

5301 Alpha Rd,

Suite 80 #200

Dallas, TX 75240

www.brimingstone.press

Book and Cover design by Brimingstone Press

ISBN: 978-1-953562-02-9

Table of Contents

"The arc of the moral universe is long, but it bends toward justice."

-   Martin Luther King, Jr.

Chapter One

Everything seemed so bright. Yet it took him only a few seconds to understand where he was. A hospital bed, and he heard the constant beeping of a heart rate monitor. He ached all over and he felt nauseous, but while he was able to move every limb in his body, his muscles felt like burning when he tried to shift.

What in the world, he thought. A million questions filled his mind, as he tried to acclimate himself to his present situation. He heard footsteps approaching.

A nurse had come inside to check on him and she gasped with excitement.

"Oh my god, he's awake!" she exclaimed and immediately hit the intercom.

Within no time, the doctor had come, flanked by two other nurses. The doc checked his pupils, asked if he knew where he was.

"A hospital bed?" Aside from that, he had no clue.

It was enough to elicit chuckle from the staff. But then the doc asked him what day it was.

"Tuesday?"

"It's Wednesday. What date?"

"July 2nd, 2006?" It was the last date he could remember.

"Son, it's June 1st, 2018."

He was in shock for a moment. Wait, this couldn't be real. This was an elaborate prank, set up by his buddies. He quickly dove deeper into his mind try and remember who these buddies were and couldn't remember any names. He couldn't even remember his own name, try as he might. His brain seemed to have such a haze that it was a miracle he could remember what a hospital was, let alone how to talk.

"You've been in a coma for 12 years," the doctor explained.

There was a groan from the patient, whose eyes widened with incredulity and bewilderment.

"I know, I know, that's a lot to process, but we're here to help you. Do you remember who you are? What is your name?" the doc asked calmly. He had good bedside manner.

"I—I can't remember."

The patient began to look flustered, and he squinted his eyes in an effort to search the back of his mind for answers. His heart rate began to go up.

"That's okay, do you mind if we call you JD? That's what me and the staff have been referring to you as. You have no identification records with us. I'm Doctor Martin, and I'm actually the fourth doctor that has been assigned to you through your stay here."

"JD" nodded silently, but it was obvious he was in shock. He couldn't remember who he was, but he seemed able to remember most everything else. He remembered how to move, and he was eager to get out of that bed. He then tried to do so, much to the vexation of the staff, who had to calm him down.

The rest of the week was spent undergoing several tests, both physically and psychologically, perhaps to ensure that his recovery was complete, and he had passed, much to his surprise. To him, everything seemed normal, except for the fact he couldn't remember certain things, and it felt like he had merely fast-forwarded into the future. There was just so much he had to catch up on. Doc

Martin had given a diagnosis of *retrograde amnesia*, but aside from that, nothing else was found wrong with him. This was a testament to the competency of the caretaking staff.

Still, it was unusual. He knew most coma survivors weren't able to regain their former physical abilities, even if their brain recovered. And those that did usually took months, even years of rehab and therapy. Yet it was like something, someone, needed him. The feeling persisted, yet he could not logically explain it. Regardless, he was still a long way from being fully normal, and knowing who he truly was, was only the first step.

Whatever had put him into a coma didn't affect the rest of his body. Doc Martin said his records indicated head trauma. He was supposed to talk to the clerk to find out more, and he was ecstatic to just be walking around without issue before he found himself sitting in the clerk's office, waiting for his turn.

"Patient John Doe," the clerk called.

So that's where "JD" comes from.

"I guess that's me," JD responded and approached the desk. "I've been cleared for release."

The clerk looked at him incredulously.

"You're the one in that coma for twelve years?"

"Yes, ma'am."

The clerk shook her head. "Incredible. Well, congratulations. If Doc Martin says you're good to go, you're good to go." Other than that, she didn't seem further impressed.

She continued, "I have to let you know, according to our records you were brought in here on the verge of death in 2006. We have no record of who you are, and all our attempts to access databases to assess your identity were blocked. Law enforcement has told over the years that they, too, have been blocked when analyzing biometric records."

Very strange, JD thought. So *who am I?*

"I'm sure you're eager to go out and see what's changed over the years. I've been instructed to not ask any questions and hand you your stuff," the clerk said. She reached into a drawer and retrieved a large yellow envelope. "Oh, and your hospital bill has been covered."

What?

"Really?" JD asked, wide eyed. He could not believe it. Twelve years of non-stop care could not have been cheap. He began to suspect government involvement. Still, nothing came to memory to hint at this. He knew the hospital wouldn't have all the answers. He would have to piece together the mystery by himself.

He was initially speechless, but managed to say, "Thank you," as he accepted the package and exited the office. As he rounded the hall, he tore open the enveloped. Inside was a stack of cash. His mouth fell agape. He had wondered how he was going to restart his life again, and before he knew it, he had it handed to him on a silver platter. Well, a yellow envelope, but it might as well have been a silver platter.

He darted into a restroom and ducked into a stall. Out of prying eyes, he eagerly counted the cash. There were fifty $100 bills, amounting to $5,000. It was enough to get him somewhere. There were also a set of keys in the envelope. One key looked like a car key, the other he wasn't sure. The only other item in the envelope was a business card. It was not your usual card, as it was made of metal. On it was etched a number.

Fascinating.

Feeling intrigued, he wanted to call the number to see if he could get some answers. He would need some, as everything was hazy in his mind. He tried to think hard until finally as he closed his eyes he could remember—he was running in a field. Towards where and from where he could not discern. The sun was setting in some trees, some rays of the sun seeping through the foliage creating dots of light upon the grass he was sprinting over. Then nothing.

Nothing at all.

Frustrated, he stood up and promptly exited the restroom after securing the cash, keys and card in his pockets and trashing the envelope. He made his way back to his former room, hoping to still catch Doc Martin and the staff to thank them for the years of taking care of him. Finally seeing his room number, he opened the door and ran into—total darkness.

Chapter Two

Strange.

Suddenly the lights came on. Ugh. JD squinted his eyes.

"Surprise!!" a chorus of voices exclaimed.

Doc Martin, the nurses who took care of him who he now knew as Emily and Joy were there. A dozen other hospital staff had crowded in the room for a send-off. Doc Martin spoke first.

"JD, I know you probably don't realize it, but you've been a great source of inspiration for all of us because of your recovery," the graying physician remarked. "While all you did was basically lay there for years, we've monitored your brain activity and noticed very gradual improvements. Until…just this past week your brain activity jumped up the scale immensely."

"Thanks, doc," JD replied, sheepishly. "But all the credit goes to you and your team. I hope this celebration isn't for me, because it really is for all of you guys."

He eyed Emily, who smiled at him. *Was she still single?* She didn't wear a ring. The staff took turns patting him on the back, sharing stories with him about the times they thought he was improving enough to wake up. In fact, the nurses had put up a little bet as to whose shift he would return to consciousness on. Apparently, that honor went to Joy.

JD felt he should be offended at being the subject of a wager, but he took all it in good fun. He was just glad to be alive and back in the world of the living so-to-speak, and if the staff did as good a job as they did, they deserved a little fun. After all, this room would now be made available for another patient.

Non-alcoholic fizzy drinks were being passed around, and JD sampled the raw-veggie-and-ranch-dip platter more than a few times. He approached Emily. She was about an inch shorter than him, blonde with long curls. She was cute, and her smile made him blush.

"Say, Emily," JD began. "I'd like to thank you for your care. How long have you been on the staff assigned to me?"

"Eight months," Emily responded. "And, no need to thank me, I was just doing my job."

"Still, I'd like to express my gratitude."

"You're too sweet, JD."

"Maybe I could treat you to dinner, sometime? As part of my saying thanks." JD looked hopeful.

"That's nice of you, JD, but we have a strict policy here to avoid the Florence Nightingale effect," Emily chuckled. It sounded like she was only half serious. She took a sip of her fizzy but didn't look like she wanted to avoid him.

"You won't get rid of me easily, miss, and technically, I'm not even a patient here anymore, so…what do you say?" JD was surprised at how bold he was.

"Well okay, but I don't get a day off for another week. Call me then?" Emily took a sticky note, took a pen and wrote down her number. She handed it to him, smiled, then turned around to mingle with her co-workers.

Making fast friends.

Doc Martin approached. Then he clapped his hands loudly to get everyone's attention. Silence filled the room. The doctor cleared his throat.

"JD is right, this celebration is not just for him, but a big congratulatory for all of the staff here that worked on his case. We all know how hard it will be for him to get back on his feet after so long. He has no relatives on record, and we don't know who he is. Unfortunately, the amnesia means he doesn't know either."

There was silence in the room as Dr. Martin turned to face JD.

"So, JD, the staff and I had decided to do something we haven't yet done for a patient. We've arranged a collection, and everyone here has pitched in, and we wanted to present you with this gift that we hope will help you find the answers you are looking for."

The smiling Emily came up and approached. There were a few who had witnessed their exchanged earlier teasing, "Weeew" as she came up to JD. He blushed.

"No, she's not the present," the doctor laughed. "Emily, if you will."

"JD, on behalf of your care team, we'd like to give you something to remember us by. I know you barely know us, since you only gained consciousness recently, but we all feel like we know you well. Despite your condition, you kept fighting, and returned to the land of the living. We wanted to give you something that will help you find out who you are."

Emily held up a box to JD. He smiled and took it as the staff applauded. He carefully removed the tape and opened the box and inside was the sleekest laptop computer he had ever seen. It looked like something from the future. Well, it was the future. Everyone applauded again and came up to pat him on the back or shake his hand. It was a warm feeling. For now, it was the closest thing he had to a family.

He later found himself in a hallway, laptop tucked into a backpack a staff member had given him. The gift giving didn't stop with the laptop. Doc Martin had given him a prepaid phone, paid for a month. He was fascinated with how fast, thin and large the phone was for a prepaid. Doc was on speed dial, and he could call him at any time he needed. Technology had advanced in leaps and bounds over the last twelve years and he was eager to find out how much other things had changed. It was a good thing the hospital staff was helping him out. They were all too generous.

But now he had a mystery to uncover. He needed to know who he was. Why was he in a coma? And who left him the money and the number to call? He was tempted to dial the number right away, but he determined he needed some good privacy. So, he had checked the keys he had found in the envelope, and attached to the keychain was a handwritten label, "2A". He had a hunch that this meant a parking spot in the parking garage, so after two flights of stairs he was in the second story parking garage. Sure enough, there was a car in the 2A spot. A black Toyota Camry sedan.

Let's see if this works.

JD carefully inserted the key in the hole of the driver's side door and took a breath of relief as he heard it click and he was able to turn it to unlock the door. He opened it and sat inside, sliding his belongings into the passenger's seat. He sighed then dug for the phone in his pocket.

The car seemed brand new. But it smelt of age. An ever so thin layer of dust had gathered over the dash, and he felt it had been there for years. Perhaps it was his car before he fell into a coma? No, it was unlikely he drove himself to the hospital if he had the head trauma that Doc Martin described which led to his twelve-year slumber. Someone else left it there for him. And now it was time to find out who.

He fiddled for the metal card in his pocket. It was thick enough not to cut him, and the etching upon it was neat and tidy, engraved by a laser. Now, finally with the privacy he longed for, he dialed the number and then held the phone to his ear. It rang three times before he heard a click, and there was a recording. It was a digitally distorted voice, but high pitched which he imagined to be a female or a young male.

"Please enter the code on the back of the card," the voice said.

Okaaay. This is serious stuff, JD thought.

He turned the card over and complied. There was a beep. Then momentary silence. All of a sudden, he heard,

"Code confirmed. You will receive a text message with an address. Please proceed to it directly."

He was so eager to find out who he was, he didn't hesitate to start the car. The question now was, could he remember how to drive. Well, he remembered how to walk, talk, and basic motor functions worked, and before long he had driven out of the garage and into the street.

Chapter Three

JD seemed to cruise well through the streets of Las Cruces, New Mexico, and he soon developed confidence in his abilities to get anywhere. The car almost had a full tank of gas, and he could drive for hours. But the directions on the phone seemed to point to a remote location in the desert, east of the city. As he drove, it looked like he was heading towards the Organ Mountains. He had to be cautious; he didn't have a driver's license and couldn't imagine what he'd say to a trooper if he was stopped for any reason.

He had driven for almost half an hour from the city outskirts and felt like he was getting close to the base of the mountains. But the directions said he was getting close. Before he knew it, the automated voice indicated he had reached his destination. It was very remote. Had he been here before? As he drove up to the driveway of the address to park, he tried to scan his brain for any memories of the place.

None.

When he drove through Las Cruces it was like driving through a city he had never been in before. Luckily, he had an address, and the phone maps app did the rest. The surrounding land was arid and flat, although in the near distance the Organ Mountains loomed above him. There wasn't another house in sight for miles. The last building that he passed on the way here was a good ten minutes' drive away. Whoever built this home designed it for maximum social distancing, possibly an introvert that relished time away from the crowds.

Come to think of it, he felt a bit introverted too; the party at the hospital had him exhausted, and a quiet place outside of town was a perfect place for him to go to. He grabbed his new laptop, exited the car and approached the home. It was rectangular and looked like the topside of a military-grade bunker except for the glass paneled windows all around the structure. It looked well-kept and maintained; in the center of the structure was an opening where a small oasis theme garden was there. Whoever this property belonged to was very affluent.

JD began to search his mind. Who was he before his coma? Was he rich? Famous? Well, if he was the latter, the hospital staff would have known who he was. The envelope had no name, no identifying features. But now was the opportunity to find out exactly what was going on. He needed to piece together who he was. He knew he had a purpose on this Earth. As he approached the home, he gathered in the surroundings, sight, smell and sound to detect any familiarity.

Again, none.

The afternoon sun beat down on him, with nary a cloud in the sky and he felt parched. He reached the front door which looked like it was made with reinforced glass and looked for a doorbell. He saw what looked like a little console on the side of the door to his right. It looked like a little touch screen. He tapped it and it came to life.

Woah. Neato.

The same digitized voice he heard on the phone earlier spoke.

"Please scan your key."

Key? JD dug into his pocket for the key. He was confused for a moment. He tried and tapped the key chain on the console. Nothing happened. *Okaaay.* He tried all sides of the keys he had.

"Um, it's not working?" JD said out loud as he kept tapping the key on the screen. There was no response. Frustration began to set in when had a thought. He took out the metallic card from his pocket and tapped the small screen with it. The screen immediately came alive and said, "Welcome!" There was an electronic buzz and a mechanical click, and the door was unlatched. He pulled on the handle and walked cautiously inside.

That's when his extra senses kicked on. It was almost like a switch was turned on and he seemed to have abilities he couldn't remember that he had. He cut the corners of the house by side-stepping, peering around them to see if anyone if there was a threat. The home was eerily quiet, and there were very few places to hide as the house was a minimalist design, had a few pieces of furniture and very few walls.

Satisfied that there were no threats after checking potential places of cover, he walked over to the glass dining table and saw neatly stacked papers. There was also a US Passport and a New Mexico driver's license, both current. He eagerly checked them. It was his picture alright, on the IDs, and the date of birth indicated he was thirty-eight years of age. He would have been twenty-six when he fell into a coma. But it was his name that had him excited.

TOM MEADOWS.

Was this his real name? *Who cares*, he thought. It was something, an identity. Was this where he lived? Did he own this land? He shifted through the papers on the table. A deed to the house was there with his name on it. There was also a title to the car he was driving. He was set. $5,000 in cash, a house that was paid for, a car and all he needed now was a life. And that's what the confusing part was. The titles and deeds were dated two years ago, but he had been in a coma for twelve. Someone had set this all up for him. But why? A zillion theories raced through his head. Was he a government agent? Did he use to work for a multi-billion-dollar company? Was he part of a lucrative drug smuggling ring? All sorts of theories about what business he was involved in, legal and illegal came to his mind. And how was he able to think of all these theories and possibilities when he couldn't even remember his name? That amnesia business was some weird stuff.

He set the laptop on the dining table and pressed the power button and heard a hum. The laptop looked too thin to real, and it booted up very quickly. Everything was so technologically advanced!

Windows 10? What happened to Windows XP? he thought, amused. He understood everything would seem so futuristic around him, even if only twelve years had passed, there was so many advancements. But at the forefront of his mind was what his past life must have been like and who it was that was looking out for him all this time?

Maybe there were more answers somewhere in the house. *Tom*, as he now began to acclimate calling himself as, made his way to one of the very few walled off areas of the home, the master bedroom. It was huge. Complete with a walk-in closet, bathroom and a huge flat-screen TV. He strolled into the closet and noticed a safe with a console similar to the one on the front door. He tapped the screen. It came to life.

Woah.

"Please speak your name," the digitized voice said this time.

"Tom Meadows," Tom exclaimed.

"Welcome, Tom," the voice replied.

Immediately there was a mechanical whirring and a click, and Tom was able to open the safe.

So fascinating.

There was a light that illuminated the insides and he saw a handgun, specifically a SIG Sauer P320. How did he know that? He searched his mind, and he knew models of guns, and their calibers. Funny how he was able to know all that but not who he was. The doctor did say retrograde amnesia was selective in the memories lost, so that would explain the crucial gaps in many areas of his memory, but his ability to retain other parts remained. He only hoped whatever he was into in the past wasn't some shady business.

Four loaded magazines of 9mm ammunition lay neatly beside the pistol, along with a box filled with even more bullets. There was a holster that he could clip onto his belt and behind the firearm was another three stacks of cash.

So, I am given a gun. Free car, free house and piles of cash. What was I into?

Did he work for a cartel? Was he an enforcer for some drug lord? He might have lost key memories of who he was, but that moral compass of his seemed to have remained intact. He searched his inner values and found no desire to be an outlaw of any type.

I shouldn't concern myself about it now, though, everything will come back to me gradually. For now, all I want to know is whether I can shoot this thing.

He loaded the gun, strapped it to his belt and strolled into the kitchen. Parched, he opened the fridge to see if there was any cold water and found a six pack of coke cans. He took a can and downed its contents. The sugar rush made his entire body shudder, but he had an idea and took the empty can with him into the back of the house. There was nothing but flat land all around and the looming mountain range in the distance.

With a heave he threw the can in the air. There was no wind, so the aluminum cylinder traveled in an arc. He couldn't quite explain what happened next. Within a split second he had unholstered the SIG, thumbed the safety off, and fired a shot. An *aimed* shot. The soda can fell to the ground, a bullet hole right through it.

Well, what do you know? I'm a crack shot.

Chapter Four

That didn't freak him out too much. It was the fact that his mysterious benefactor knew that he knew how to handle one. But it wasn't just that he could shoot. The gun felt natural in his hand. Almost like it was a part of him.

Was I some assassin for hire?

Tom took a deep breath. He had to stop speculating. He would take everything on a day-to-day basis and try not to get ahead of himself. The puzzle will come together in time. For now, the fridge was empty besides the cans of pop he had found earlier. Time for a grocery run.

It was still a little past midday, and the heat had grown worse and worse. There was no way he was going to subsist on soda pop for the rest of the day. So, he made his way into the house and walked out the front door. As he stepped out, the door latched shut behind him, and the digitized voice said,

"Residence secured."

Cool.

He paused. He knew the keys were in his pocket, so he deduced it had a mechanism to detect that he exited the home with the card. He shrugged and continued to his car and started the engine. He unholstered his pistol and hid it underneath his seat as he pulled out of the driveway and onto the barely paved road leading back into town. He turned on the radio and searched for an appropriate station. It was then that he realized he liked classical for some reason. It was soothing and calming. The last piece of music ended, but he didn't quite catch the tune. The next one came on, which he immediately recognized as Beethoven's Symphony No. 9.

He felt it strange how he knew that but couldn't remember who he really was. Yes, he was Tom Meadows according to his identity documents, but that didn't ring a bell in his mind—yet. He still couldn't remember if that was who he really was. Someone could have just given him that identity. But for now, he wanted to enjoy the moment. He was someone besides "John Doe", although he was starting to get used to being called "JD" after spending a week in rehab.

After picking up his necessities from the store, he planned to return home, plop on the sofa with his laptop and catch up with everything that had happened in the world over the past twelve years.

After about ten minutes of driving, he only saw about two other cars on the road going the opposite direction. He was almost halfway to town when he saw a vehicle on the side of the road, with what looked like a flat tire. Two silhouettes stood by it, one significantly shorter than the other. As he neared, the desert mirage disappeared, and his vision cleared and he could clearly make out a woman, probably in her early thirties, along with a young girl.

He was immediately overcome with compassion, and so he slowed down to a halt on the side of the road and placed his Camry into park. The heat of the noon desert climate was almost overwhelming, and he wondered how long the two ladies were there waiting under the scorching sun. With no one around for what seemed like miles, he knew he had to help. He stepped out his car and slowly approached, smiling.

"Afternoon, ma'am," he said, shielding his eyes from the glaring sun. She was a couple inches shorter than him, brunette, long flowing dark hair. She had Aviator shades on which she removed as she smiled back. He detected an expression of not just relief on her face, but something else he couldn't quite pin down. Was it recognition? The woman sighed with relief while smiling like she was looking at someone she had been waiting for all her life.

"Hey, thanks for stopping!" she exclaimed. She was still smiling.

Well, heat like this can make people do some strange things.

Tom extended his hand.

"I'm Tom, I live just a few miles down the road. I saw you and your little one out here in this heat, I knew I couldn't just drive by," he said.

She shook his hand.

"I'm Lina, Lina Edwards. And this is my seven-year-old, Elizabeth. Liz, say hi," Lina placed her arm around her daughter, as the young girl flashed a toothless smile.

"Hi, Mister Tom," Elizabeth said, shyly.

Tom stooped down near her height to shake her hand.

"Hi Miss Elizabeth," he said gently, looking into her gleaming eyes as he shook her hand. "I'll be helping you and your mom get this tired fixed so you can be on your way."

"Thank you, Tom," Lina exclaimed, breathing a sigh a relief. "We've been here for almost an hour."

"You're welcome."

As Lina told Elizabeth a story, the child giggled. Tom went to work jacking up the car and removing the flat tire. It seemed so routine he was constantly fascinated at how much he was still able to remember to do, all things considered. It was like he fell asleep a day ago, then woke up, all his memories intact except the parts he felt that mattered, such as who he was, and what he did for a living.

All-in-all it took him less than ten minutes to replace the tire, and the spare was on firmly and ready to go. He put away the tools and rubbed his hands together to rub off the dirt and grime. He approached Lina.

"You're good to go, Lina," he said, and then turned to Elizabeth, "You're all ready to go, sweetie."

"Yay!" the young girl exclaimed and opened the car door to climb into her car seat.

Tom stood smiling as Lina turned her engine on to get the AC running. She shut the door and turned back to approach him. A gust of desert wind blew their way and pushed her flowing hair behind her. She was a stunning woman. Tom's heart was racing as he beheld a beauty like he had never seen before. He was confused as to why he was so smitten. The nurse Emily was a fine lass, yet there was something about Lina that took him to another world even with just her smile. Still, he was determined to be the quintessential gentleman and professional, and he reminded himself he was there to help and not to flirt.

While she was an attractive woman, Lina had an air of authority, which seemed somewhat intimidating to him. Besides, she was likely already married to whoever Elizabeth's father might be, although he saw no ring. He was also looking forward to taking Emily out the following week. But something about Lina intrigued him.

"Tom, I don't know how to thank you," Lina began. "You're our hero."

"Ah, it was nothing," Tom replied, hoping he wouldn't be seen blushing. "I couldn't leave a mother and her daughter in distress out here, especially in this heat."

"Well, that's very kind and sweet of you," Lina smiled. "Please, let me return the favor. Elizabeth and I would love to have you over for dinner. I can cook you a hot homemade meal. What do you say?"

"I can't possibly intrude upon—"

"Please, we insist," Lina reached out to touch his arm. "It's just me and her. I'm a single mother, and we've had no one around for dinner for a long time."

"Are you, er, sure, Lina?"

"What do you mean?"

"I'm a stranger, some random guy you are inviting in your house," Tom lowered his voice to a whisper as to not let Elizabeth hear.

"Nonsense," Lina laughed. "You're a new friend with a heart big enough to stop and render some help."

"Well, if you insist, I'd be happy to. I don't have any other plans for the day."

"Thank you. You can follow me, our house is not quite inside of town, and it's only a ten-minute drive south."

"I'll be right behind you guys," Tom replied, trying to hide his excitement. He knew by this time he was blushing red. Something about

Lina's touch made an impact on him although he didn't know why. He climbed back into his car and in moments was following Lina's vehicle down the road. Well, now he knew she was single. For some reason her voice was so soothing and calming to him, and he felt relaxed in her presence.

She's just an attractive lass, he thought to himself. For the moment, Emily was forgotten, and a smitten Tom now had the biggest smile. It was an opportunity, if not for romantic companionship, at least for a friendship, one he knew he would need as he sought to piece his life together again. She was well dressed, and her car was a Lexus—not bad for a single mother, without a husband and co-parent. She would have had to be the breadwinner of the house. Unless there was an unseen benefactor or inheritance that she benefitted from, she was doing well all on her own.

They were closer to Las Cruces now, with its outskirts visible in the near distance, but the house they were pulling up to was still remote. The neighbors were a bit closer though, separated by a few minutes' walk rather than a few minutes' drive. The house itself was gated with an automated gate and he could see several cameras installed. It felt more like a security compound rather than a residence.

For all the precautions Lina took in securing her house, she seemed too trusting. After all, they just met less than an hour ago, and now she was inviting him into her secure home. Tom knew himself—maybe not his past life, but at that moment he knew he had a moral compass, and he was determined to respect and protect. It felt like part of his nature. He parked behind Lina's vehicle and emerged from his car. The front area was kept tidy, and there was a small fountain and little fishpond and several desert plants neatly landscaped. Lina and Elizabeth emerged from their car and made their way inside the home.

"Come on in," Lina called out. "I want you to feel at home."

Tom nodded and followed. He made sure to keep his distance and look non-assuming. This made him tense and uncomfortable. Sure, he needed friends, but he expected to win trust a little more gradually. But he was thankful for Lina's trust. Or maybe her high reliance on technological security gave her the confidence. Either way, he was determined to win her trust over completely.

Chapter Five

The dinner was delicious. Lina was a world class cook. He had a lot of questions, but he started with the basics. She was thirty-five years old, a software executive. This explained her wealth. She had been in the industry for almost eight years now, as Chief Executive Officer. She talked about Elizabeth, how she was the love of her life. She didn't talk about the father, only that she was engaged two years before her daughter was born and didn't end up married.

Tom didn't want to come across as prying, so he declined to pursue the matter further, even if he was very curious about it. He did muster up the courage to ask her what company she worked for.

"Gensoft Systems Incorporated," she replied.

Gensoft? Tom ears perked up. Where had he heard that name before? It was in the back of his mind, but he couldn't remember why.

"Me… and a colleague of mine founded the company, and well, we've been booming in business since. We host a programming platform to provides interfaces for mobile apps for our clients," Lina continued. "It's a lucrative business, but despite all the money it doesn't necessarily win you many friends as you can see. Mostly I am inside, doing much of my work online."

She went on to explain she did almost half of the programming work for the company, and that there were twenty-one other employees, all of them working from home as well. Tom listened intently, even if he felt more intimidated the more she rattled off her credentials and experience. Lina was definitely out of his league. But as long as she would have him around, he was happy to have and give company. Then, she turned the conversation around and began to ask him questions.

"So, Tom. How about you, can you tell me more about yourself?" Lina asked, interlocking her fingers together as she placed her hands on the table while leaning forward, smiling.

Uh oh.

This was the moment he dreaded. What was he going to say? Should he make up some story? Or tell her the truth? He was silent for a few moments as he debated himself in his mind. He could lie, but then he would have come up with a backstory quick, and should their relationship formulate into a friendship, he would have to continue lying. This wasn't something he was ready to do. Besides, Lina was trusting enough to let him in her home, and he couldn't betray that trust by lying. He had just returned to the world of consciousness and didn't know who he could trust. But he decided in this case, he would repay trust with trust.

"I—I actually don't know much about myself," he blurted out, after what seemed like forever. "I didn't even know what had been happening in the world before the other week."

He must have looked distressed, because Lina reached over the table to touch his hand. He looked down at his empty plate. He was going to bare his soul to this woman. She looked concerned, and he hoped it wasn't because she was thinking he had some mental issue.

"Okay," Lina responded softly. "It's okay," she assured. "Help me understand."

Tom sat back, took a deep breath and let it out slowly.

"Yesterday I was released from the hospital after a week of rehab. Before that, apparently, I was in a deep coma for twelve years," he explained. "I have retrograde amnesia and I don't even know if Tom is my real name. I just found documents in the house I was left keys for in my hospital belongings. I can remember how to do pretty much everything I used to, and I remember things that I like, but memories relating to events and things that happened before I fell into a coma were lost. It's strange, but my doctor said this isn't necessarily unusual since certain memories can be affected when only certain areas of the brain are damaged.

"I know I just met you, but I'm opening up with my everything because I have no one else to go to. I don't even know who I was before all this."

He took a breath then held it as he waited for her reaction. He half expected her to throw him out of the house and tell him not to come back. Instead, she kept leaning forward, listening to his every word. She had a look of concern on her face. After he finished, she remained silent for at least a minute.

"Excuse me," she finally said, then stood up and left to enter a door, presumably a bathroom.

Way to go, Tomster. You creeped her out.

After another minute, she emerged, sniffling. She sat back down.

"Sorry," she said. "Allergies."

"No problem. Listen, I know it might be all strange for you, I mean, we just met," Tom expressed as he stood up. "It might be best if I be on my way."

"Tom," Lina stood up as well. "don't go."

She had an expression of sadness in her eyes.

"I've never met as honest a man like you in my life," she said. "I know it was hard for you to express to me what you just did. Someone else would have told some lie and make up a story."

Tom stared at the floor. He felt an incredible urge to run out. But something kept him glued in place. Something about Lina. She was almost too kind, too trusting. But it also calmed him and allowed him to trust and open up in return.

He found a friend he would be loyal to. And deep within, his system of values told him he would be exactly that. After what seemed forever, he finally opened up.

"Thank you, Lina," he said, looking back up and staring into her dark, kind eyes, "but how do you know I'm not just telling some sob story."

"We needed help and you stopped to help us," she said, smiling. "Besides, the story you told me was too incredible to be a sob story. I could come up with any number of better stories than that. So, either you are a horrible, horrible storyteller, or you are telling the truth."

Tom had to laugh. It was the first time he had done so in a real tangible manner since waking up from the coma. He could only stand there, staring at the woman he just met, who captivated him in every single way imaginable. If he didn't know any better, he'd have said he was in love, but they've only known each other for a little under two hours.

"Thank you for dinner, Lina. It was delicious. I consider your debt paid," Tom joked, extending his hand. "I had a wonderful time, and I hope you have me back."

"Certainly, Tom. I want you to come back," Lina said as she walked towards him. But instead of taking his hand she came closer and embraced him. He thought that he should have felt awkward, but he didn't. He returned her embrace. Cozy. Warm. A thousand different thoughts raced through his head.

Finally, she released him, after what he thought was initial reluctance, and he cleared his throat. It was now time to actually get to the store and get what he needed. He and Lina exchanged numbers and he said goodbye to her and Elizabeth, and within minutes he was at the local grocers. But every moment he was there, he couldn't take Lina Edwards off his mind.

Chapter Six

The phone was vibrating. Tom yawned as he rolled over in bed, feeling for his phone. *Where is that thing.* He finally found it under his pillow, and he squinted his eyes to look at the screen. It was still dark outside. Phone said 2:12 AM. *Who is calling at this hour?* The phone vibrated again.

LINA EDWARDS

Oh, it's Lina. What might be wrong that she would call this early?

He pressed the receive call button on the screen. He heard Lina's voice, shaky, scared.

"Tom?"

"Lina! Is everything okay?"

"I'm so sorry for bothering you," Lina said, "but I had no one else to call."

Silence.

"Lina? What's going on?"

"Okay. I didn't tell you yesterday because I didn't want to overwhelm or scare you. But the last few months, thugs have tried to break into my house."

"What!?"

"Yes. And tonight, they tried again, this time taking one of my security cameras offline."

"Have you tried to call the police?"

Silence again.

"Lina? Are you there?"

"Listen, Tom, there's something I need to tell you. I can't call the police."

"Why?" Tom asked, confused.

"I—I can't talk over the phone."

A stunned Tom was quiet for a moment. He didn't know what to make of all of it, but he was wide awake now. He wanted to head over to Lina's right away.

"Okay, hang in there, I'll be over in a few minutes," Tom said, hanging up as he rushed to change.

It took him no more than ten minutes to get there, when it ordinarily should have taken fifteen. He felt like he was flying instead of driving. Doing a quick scouting run around the perimeter after parking, he noticed nothing amiss, and then rang the doorbell. He heard footsteps approach the door.

"Lina, it's me, Tom," he said assuredly, but the door was already open by then. A disheveled looking Lina smiled in recognition and hugged him tightly.

"I know, Tom. I still have a few other cameras working," she pointed out. "Thank God you're here!"

Lina led Tom to her couch and they both sat down. Tom looked very concerned, and he asked Lina to explain what was going on. It was a narrative that would make anyone cringe and took almost a full hour to express. Lina believed the perpetrators were gang members protected by the local Chief of Police. She had done some research and found that an uptick in crime was caused by the local gang the Las Cruces Tridents. Police Chief Garth Ohlgren had suspiciously released twenty of their members from custody and fired two officers who were involved in their arrests.

Chief Ohlgren, in his position and stature, was almost unassailable. His publicly known record was clean, and even the county commissioners saw only good marks and service. But rumors went around. Lina explained that she never placed faith in rumors;

however, things started to add up. Ohlgren would be missing from crucial Law Enforcement meetings according to a friend of hers that worked for the city. And there was the spate of mysterious disappearances, mostly young women, and when reported to the police, there was no movement, or anything tangible in the way of police investigating, causing frustration in affected families.

Lina was convinced the gang was involved, and that Ohlgren was protecting them for some reason. She couldn't prove it, but everything she uncovered so far pointed at Ohlgren.

"So, you see, Tom, I can't call the police. And every day that passes makes them bolder. I got a call from a friend on the other side of town last week, she said her windows were smashed and she called the police. They came and told her to file an insurance claim and that was it! Can you believe it?"

Tom shook his head in disbelief.

"That stinks. You don't know who to trust," he responded.

"Exactly," Lina said. "I know…" her voice drifted off a little. "I know I barely know you, but I would just as soon trust you than the police at the moment."

"Thank you," Tom smiled warmly as he replied. "I promise you I will reward that trust. But for now, go and get yourself some rest."

He stood and gently took Lina's hand to assist her off the couch.

"Good night, Lina. Rest well."

"Good night, Tom. Thank you for being here."

Lina retired to her room, and Tom looked at his watch. 3:44 AM. For the next two hours, Tom vigilantly stood guard near the front door of the house, armed with his SIG. Elizabeth was upstairs in her own room, sleeping soundly. He only had managed to sit silently, fully alert for the full two hours. He also felt his senses were heightened. He analyzed every sound he heard, carefully watched for any movement outside that would indicate trouble. But there was nothing.

Lina awoke around at around 6 AM, and she began to make breakfast. Elizabeth was about to go to school, Lina explained, and Tom could go home if he wanted to.

"I'll make my way home," Tom explained, "but please call me immediately if anything happens."

Lina nodded, gave him a tight hug, and Tom waved goodbye to Elizabeth before leaving. He was uncomfortable leaving, but he knew he had a long way to go before suggesting he move in with them. Besides, he had his own home to take care of. Twenty minutes later he was back home, on the couch watching the news. He also had his laptop open, reading world news reports going back to 2007.

He found himself going back a bit further, as there were things he couldn't remember even in the early 2000's. He remembered 9-11 but remembered very little afterwards. As he tried to access key memories in his mind, he would suffer a headache. It was all too overwhelming, so after a few minutes, he closed his laptop shut and hit the remote power button to switch off the TV. He sighed and plopped onto the sofa. He was about to doze off when his phone vibrated again.

Lina.

He quickly fumbled for the phone and answered it, without looking at the number.

"Lina!?"

"Mr. Meadows," the familiar digitized voice said, "please turn on the television."

What, now?

There was a click at the end of the other line, then silence. He hung up.

Okay.

He picked up the remote and switched the TV on again. This time the news channel was not on, but a black screen with a logo. He didn't recognize the logo. He waited and a couple seconds later the screen transitioned to what looked like a slideshow presentation. There were pictures and captions. He had never seen these individuals before, but the pictures showed news articles, and the captions made it clear who they were. It was obvious that they were bigshots in law enforcement for the city of Las Cruces.

Chief Ohlgren was there, holding an award of sorts on a plaque. There were also businessmen. Tony Murdock, a multi-million-dollar car dealership owner was prominently shown, shaking hands with Chief Ohlgren. News articles flashed on the screen, showing the accomplishments of each individual. Then the slideshow changes its presentation.

This time, no captions, no articles. Just pictures of the previously mentioned men. Ohlgren, Murdock, and a dozen others, in surveillance photos. It wasn't clear who took the photos. But they showed the men with each other, and their meetings in secret locations with shady looking people. Some in street clothes, others in business suits, but with civilian bodyguards toting automatic rifles.

In one picture, there was a picture of Ohlgren, in civilian clothes, his arm around a man, they seemed jovial, laughing at something. The next picture shocked him. The man whom Ohlgren was with, was pictured pulling a girl from a car. The girl was blindfolded, and her hands were tied together.

Tom's blood began to boil. If the police chief was truly involved with this man who was taking young girls for who knows what, he had to be dealt with. Another picture flashed, and this time it was Murdock, who stood enjoying a cigar and laughing with the same man. Tom felt his neck tense up. His blood pressure was rising.

The screen then flashed newspaper articles of families missing children. A missing 8-year-old. A 15-year-old. A 12-year-old. How sick can these people be? Tom thought, angry, feeling ready to rip someone's throat out. He switched the television off. He couldn't take it anymore. Something had to be done. Call the police? Feds? That notion was laughable at this point. Investigations could take months, even years, and in the meantime, girls would disappear. The monsters had to be stopped. At this point, the only one who could do anything about it was…him.

He opened his laptop and conducted a quick search. Within seconds, addresses appeared. He vetted the names and by process of elimination found what he was looking for, the address for Anthony Ervin Murdock. He entered it in his phone, changed his clothes to a black button-down and blue jean, and was soon outside and in the car. He reached underneath the seat to feel the cold metal of the SIG.

Tony, I'm coming for 'ya.

Chapter Seven

Murdock's residence was on the other side of town to the west. It was in a rich, gated community, not unlike many other millionaires. Tom drove up slowly to the gate guardhouse and a guard came out who just checked his ID, wrote in a notebook and opened the gate without asking any further questions. It was too easy.

He drove right up to the home, which was protected by a wall and another gate. It looked huge. He couldn't see over the wall, but he imagined a pool, several millionaire amenities and probably a dozen cars. But that was speculation, and now he had a problem of how to get Murdock out to confront him. Maybe he wasn't even there.

His heart was pounding as he hid his SIG compact in the small of his back. Then he stepped outside to approach the intercom in an attempt to get someone to open the gate. Before he could walk ten feet, he heard a voice behind him.

"Hey there," a man called to him.

Tom turned around. A casually dressed, middle-aged man with a mustache approached him. There was something about him that screamed "cop", even though he was in civilian garb. Maybe it was the swagger or the fact his aviator sunglasses were oversized. And he was chewing gum. Annoying.

"I'm Nick Hunter," the man said as he held out his hand. "Nice day, isn't it?"

"I'm Tom Meadows," Tom replied as he shook the man's hand, "and yes, it's quite lovely."

"Follow me," Hunter's lowered his voice to a whisper. "I have a feeling I know what you're after."

Eh? How does he know?

In any case, Tom was going to go ahead and play along. There was little chance he could have gotten into Murdock's residence anyway. He needed to come up with a plan first. But for now, he was going to hear this Nick Hunter out, and see what he was offering. He followed Hunter to a car on the other side of the road. Hunter entered the driver's side and motioned for Tom to sit in the passenger's side. Tom decided to comply. Hunter shut his door and so did Tom. Hunter removed his sunglasses and dug in his breast pocket and took out a badge.

I knew it.

"Detective Nicholas Hunter, Las Cruces Police Department."

"Wow, could I get one of those too?"

"Aw cut it out," Hunter snapped, annoyed. "Listen. I bet you're here because you've heard that Murdock is a nasty piece of work."

"Oh?" Tom replied. "How do you know I wasn't here to get an autograph?"

"Whatever, Tom. I know what you're up to. I'm a detective, I can smell intentions a mile away," Hunter said. "But I'm warning you to just let it go. We know about those nasty rumors you heard about, and we've been keeping Murdock under twenty-four-seven surveillance and you doing your thing will only jeopardize our investigation."

For some reason, Tom wasn't convinced. But he decided to play along. He pretended to be deep in thought for a whole minute before sighing and responding.

"Yeah. You're right, Nick. My apologies. I'll let you guys handle this. But you keep me updated, you hear? A friend's niece has been missing for two years already, and I can't help but think this bastard had something to do with it," he lied. "I'd like to know if he truly is responsible."

Hunter laughed.

"Relax. Rumors are rumors. Besides, how do you know your friend's niece didn't just run away? We get dozens of these reports each month, and each time these girls seem to return home after some time."

Oh really? Tom thought.

"We're just following up on a lead here, Tom, very routine. And I hope you haven't been listening also to those rumors of our police chief being involved in some crime syndicate."

Hunter continued to talk between chewing, much to Tom's chagrin.

"Chief Ohlgren is an honorable man. He's the one who ordered this stakeout on Murdock. Again, routine stuff. Don't believe everything you read on the internet. Rich and powerful men get accused of many things, just because they have money or position," the detective said as he popped another piece of gum in his mouth and continued chewing. "Do yourself a favor. Go home, drink a beer and let us handle this. Here."

Hunter handed Tom a business card with his name and number with the logo of the Las Cruces Police Department. Tom reckoned it was his time to leave. There was nothing more he could do here. He did not know yet what to make of Hunter's assertions. He found it strange that Nick would volunteer information that Ohlgren was not involved in any criminal activity. Sloppy for a detective, and certainly raised red flags. But Tom still needed more solid proof.

So far, all the evidence he had were the pictures. Could they have been doctored to make him think Ohlgren was corrupt? His mysterious benefactor certainly wanted him to think so. But could he trust his benefactor, or was it possible that Nick Hunter was actually telling the truth? He was thoroughly confused.

Tom decided not to investigate further at that moment, then walked back to his car, and without further delay, drove away. It was an episode he wished he could forget, just like his past, but unfortunately, he could not forget the pictures he saw. Something was going on, and eventually he was going to get at the bottom of it. He had the impulse to drive to Lina's, which he followed. The sun had already set, and he was hungry by the time he reached Lina's gate. He pressed the button on the intercom. There was a click.

"Yes?" Lina's voice came through the speaker.

"It's Tom."

"Tom! Come on in!"

The gate opened, and in moments he was parked and at the doorway. Lina opened the door and gave him a warm hug.

"You're just in time, dinner's ready."

Dinner consisted of pasta, garlic bread and some greens, and it was delicious. Elizabeth was the first to finish her meal, and at her mother's behest, she was upstairs taking a shower and getting ready for bed. While she did that, Tom helped Lina clean up. By the time they were done, Elizabeth was fast asleep. The two adults were left alone together, on the living room couch.

"Tom…" Lina began. "I can't express how relieved I am to have you around. I feel much safer with you here. Elizabeth too."

"I'm privileged to protect you two," Tom responded, looking deep into her eyes. He felt a growing connection, and he knew he had fallen for her. Lina must have felt the same too, because all of a sudden, she then grabbed him by the collar and kissed him, passionately. Tom felt blissful and reciprocated, his heart pounding. Her lips were warmly sensual, and he felt a pleasurable tingling sensation up his spine.

It seemed like forever, but it might have been just a couple minutes, since both had to pause to gasp for air. Lina backed up.

"I—I'm sorry," she said, her face seemed twisted with pain. "I'm so sorry. I can't."

"Don't be sorry," Tom replied. "You don't need to. I understand."

A tear fell down Lina's face and she hugged him tightly. He held her securely, resisting the temptation to ask what was wrong. The simple answer would be that she just wasn't ready. Whether it was past trauma, moral conviction, or some other reason, Tom just had to deal with it. For now, he just needed to be as understanding as he could. It was getting late, and after holding each other for almost an hour, Lina got up, kissed Tom on the forehead, and headed to her bed. Tom insisted on sleeping on the couch, just in case any intruders came again.

The night was uneventful, however. Morning came and Lina woke up first, preparing breakfast. Tom joined her and Elizabeth at the table half an hour later, and they were having a good time, laughing.

It feels good to have a family, Tom thought. He knew there was nothing official, but he was thankful for what he had.

Not long after that, Lina had to drop Elizabeth off at the school. Tom then made his way back home, eager to continue his research into Murdock and Ohlgren.

Chapter Eight

His research didn't yield anything conclusive, but one particular case seemed to intrigue him. The case of Maria Sanchez from south Las Cruces. Missing for two years already, and twelve-years-old when she was reported missing, she was last known to be at a friend's house down the street from where she lived. With evening nearing, she had told her friends family she was going to walk home alone, which was not unusual as she had done it several times. However, this time, she never made it home.

There were no witnesses, but on that day a police patrol car was doing rounds in the neighborhood. The patrolmen, when interviewed said they didn't notice anything unusual, and there were no disturbances that day. The family was sure they saw something or were perhaps even involved. Maria was not one to go with strangers, and if someone tried to take her from the street, she was taught to raise a ruckus.

Given that everybody knew everyone in that neighborhood, the family felt it was unlikely she was abducted forcefully. No strangers were reported in the vicinity that day. She must have gone with her abductors willingly. This is apparently when the rumors really swelled around Ohlgren and the Las Cruces police department. Relatives and friends of the Sanchez's protested outside the police station last year, maintaining that if the police were not involved, they were certainly withholding information. There was no real proof, however, and for the most part, public confidence in local law enforcement was still high.

So, Tom decided to visit the family for answers. A quick search returned a series of addresses, and with the process of elimination he selected the one that fit the profile, a residence belonging to a Ricardo Sanchez. It was not a far drive. In fact, Tom was able to make it within twenty minutes. The neighborhood itself was not run down, as the news reports suggested. These were middle-class homes and didn't look like the place gangs hung around in at all.

He knocked on the door. Dogs barked from within. A minute later, the door opened, and a man emerged, dark, slightly graying hair, Hispanic, with a goatee. He was in his late forties. *Ricardo Sanchez.*

"Ricardo Sanchez?" Tom asked.

"Yes? Who's asking?" Ricardo inquired, folding his arms together in distrust.

"My name is Tom Meadows, and I'm a private investigator. I'm here to ask about Maria's disappearance."

"You're not with the police?"

"No sir."

"How can I know that."

"I can't prove I'm not, but what I can tell you is that I've read about Maria's disappearance and I want to help," Tom pleaded. "You don't even have to pay me."

"I don't know who to trust these days, you know?" Ricardo responded. "My daughter has been missing for two years already. Private eyes come by all the time and I always turn them down. They all smell like cops. Why should I make an exception for you?"

Just then Tom's phone rang. He took it out of his pocket and answered it.

"Hello?" Tom said.

The familiar digitized voice replied and instructed him to give the phone to Ricardo. He was confused. But he had learned it wasn't his place to ask questions when it came to his benefactor, so he decided to comply. He held the phone out to Ricardo.

"Someone wants to talk to you," Tom told him.

Ricardo had a confused look but took the phone anyway.

"This is Ricardo," he said.

Tom couldn't hear what the person on the other side of the line was saying. But Ricardo kept nodding his head, and then after a minute said, "Thank you." Then he hung up and gave the phone back to Tom.

"Okay, Mr. Meadows, it looks like I can trust you. Come on inside."

Tom went inside, and Ricardo sat him on the sofa and offered a drink, which Tom declined. For the next hour, Ricardo talked about Maria, his daughter, the young, talented and intelligent girl, now nowhere to be found. He also went over the events of that day, now more than two years ago. He also expressed how he was convinced the police were either covering up or even directly involved in her abduction. He couldn't prove it, but he hoped Tom would be able to uncover some answers.

"Do you have a daughter, Mr. Meadows?" Ricardo asked.

"No sir, I do not. But I have someone who is very close to a daughter to me," Tom replied. He could imagine Elizabeth's toothless smile, and it brought a feeling of warmth to his heart. Just then his phone rang again.

"Hello?"

"Tom!! Oh Tom!!" the voice on the other line was almost screaming. It was Lina, and she was hysterical. "They have her. The bastards, they took her!"

"Lina, baby, okay, just breathe. Who has who?"

"THEY TOOK ELIZABETH! From school!"

Tom's heart stopped. He felt nauseated, and at that moment he was in a rage against whoever had kidnapped Elizabeth.

Oh, it is on. You don't want to mess with me.

He stood to his feet and told a concerned Ricardo that he needed to leave right away but would return. Sprinting as fast as he could to his car, he started the vehicle and put the metal to the floor towards Lina's place. However, he was careful not to speed too much, or risk getting pulled over and delaying his rush further. And the police were the last people he wanted to run into at the moment.

He almost ran two traffic lights, but he was at Lina's within ten minutes. He had his own access code to the gate, and he parked and rushed inside the house, holding an inconsolable Lina who was almost hysterical, crying uncontrollably on the couch. After ten minutes she finally calmed down a bit, at least enough to be able to talk and she began to tell the story.

She was working on a software project late in the morning when she received a call from Elizabeth's school, asking if there was any reason why uniformed police officers would pick her up from school. Lina instantly knew what had happened. Elizabeth had been abducted. She felt faint, and weak at the knees. A few minutes later she received a phone call from an anonymous man who claimed to be part of the Las Cruces Tridents, and told her she could not approach the police or federal law enforcement, and that she needed to pay a ransom of $4 million.

Lina revealed she had $3 million at hand but would need another two days to pull in all her investments to come close to the ransom amount. That's when Tom told her about the mysterious caller who guided him since his return to consciousness from his coma. He also told her about his shooting skills, and he told her about Maria Sanchez, and how he was going to put a stop to all this.

Lina had an idea. She just remembered that Elizabeth had a radio tracker in her shoe. Lina had a few of them installed the year before on several of her sneakers. Tom knew what he had to do. He told Lina he was going to go and get Elizabeth. Sobbing, Lina knew she had no other choice. Law enforcement wasn't going to be any help and contacting the Feds would probably endanger Elizabeth even more. While they knew there were still many in law enforcement that they could trust, they had no way of knowing *who to trust*. The bad and corrupt apples would not simply up and announce themselves.

With no time to lose, Tom left a tearful Lina to return to his house to retrieve a few more things, but not without vowing he was going to bring Elizabeth back.

There is a reckoning…and I am it.

Chapter Nine

Tom felt adrenalin rushing through his veins. He was in overdrive, and he was ready to find Elizabeth to bring her back safely, hell or high water. He had just gotten back home when his phone rang again.

What now!?

"Tom Meadows open your phone's email please," the familiar digitized voice commanded. Then there was a click, and the call was truncated. He was annoyed, but perhaps the mysterious guide had something helpful. So, he opened his email on his phone. It was from some obscure email address, and there was a link in the body of the email. He clicked the on it, and it began an app download. The app's name was INTERNODE. It took a total of four seconds to download the app, and he opened it.

"Please state your name," the digitized voice commanded.

Tom complied. He then heard a mechanical whirring in his room, so he rushed over and discovered a portion of the wall had opened like a door revealing a small room, dimly lit. Inside were racks of weapons and a self with tactical equipment. Shotguns. Automatic rifles. Pistols. Magazines and ammunition, and a black tactical vest.

Woah, he thought. *Just what I need.*

He knew what he needed to do. He picked out another SIG P320 Compact, then an M4 Colt Carbine. He donned the tactical vest, grabbed a set of binoculars and placed six full magazines of 5.56mm ammo, and several full mags of 9mm for the pistols. He was ready.

Now he just needed to know where he was headed. He needed to find a way to locate Elizabeth's tracker. Lina had mentioned the app needed to find the tracker, and Tom did a quick search, found it and installed it. He quickly opened the app. A map came up, and it loaded for a few seconds, and finally the blip showed up. It was in the southeastern portion of town, a good twenty-minute drive.

It was amazing how much technology had advanced over the past decade. Another faint memory began to surface, that of the last phone he remembered owning, a flip Motorola RAZR V3i phone. It was all the rage in his day. Now, smartphones were faster and more powerful than the last desktop computer he remembered being on the market.

He had no time to lose, so he grabbed his armament, loaded it into his car and was on his way. He began to formulate plans and ran scenarios in his head. Then he realized he was able to think tactically. More memories began to flash in his mind. Training with a combat rifle, shooting at targets and running through an obstacle course.

Tom drove past the hospital that had been his home for the last twelve years. It seemed ages ago since he left it, but it had barely been a couple of weeks. The app indicated he needed to continue east, so he steered in that direction, noticing he was driving in an area of town that had a lot of derelict homes. The app said he was only 500 meters from his destination. Half a kilometer. He would stop there and proceed on foot. There were a bunch of hills, and a lot filled with junked cars.

He exited his car, armed to the teeth, and made his way towards where the app said Elizabeth's tracker was. Then he saw it. In a clearing in the middle of several hills, an old, abandoned factory with a fence around it. In the northeastern corner he saw several cars parked, and three men standing guard. He advanced at a crouch, positioning himself to the east of the installation where he could take cover in some sand dunes and mounds of rock covered in cacti.

His phone vibrated. He received a text from the mysterious guide which stated his tactical vest had a Bluetooth earpiece. He patted around until he felt a bulge in his left breast pocket and took out the earpiece. Technology was great. Quickly, he fitted the earpiece in his ear and connected it to his phone and immediately the INTERNODE app activated.

Then what the app showed next made him sit down for a pause… it was a scan of his military ID.

Armed Forces of the United States

Marine Corps

Meadows, Tom Evan

Rank: LCPL

Then there was a copy of a dossier which showed he was part of Force Reconnaissance (FORECON) in Operation Enduring Freedom. It showed his involvement in a capture of a terrorist warlord and having earned a Purple Heart and the Navy Cross in 2004. He was a Marine. This explained his firearms proficiency. His hand-to-hand combat was an unknown; he knew Recon Marines were very combat proficient, and a few things regarding that were beginning to return to his memory. A faint glimpse of his military service days flashed briefly in his mind, but it was surrounded with so much haze, it would take a lot of mental effort and concentration to try and uncover it.

The question was not whether he knew how to fight. The question was if his body was up to it. The hospital staff did a great job in keeping his muscles toned. Using the latest electronic stimulation devices, they explained during his therapy, they were able to conduct constant therapy on his major muscle groups so they wouldn't lose their tone. It must have worked. He felt like he could wrestle an elephant, and that could come in handy if he had to come in close quarters with the Tridents.

Tom swiped the screen on his phone and the app then showed a real time video of the compound from above. It looked like his mysterious helper had a drone in the air! He couldn't hear it over the sounds of vehicles on the highway to the north, but he knew it was somewhere there.

Now he had an overwhelming tactical advantage, even if the enemy had the numbers. The earpiece cackled.

"Counting thirteen hostiles. Three in the immediate vicinity," the voice said.

Gripping the phone, Tom repositioned himself about a hundred meters from the eastern chain linked fence, near a torn-downed gate from which he could infiltrate the compound. But it would be in full view of the posted guards, so he needed to dispatch them quickly. Lifting his carbine, he adjusted the optics, which had a magnified red dot sight. Once he felt it was ready, he aimed and let loose.

The nearest guard, carrying an AK-47, had no chance. A 5.56 mm slug to the head knocked him lifeless on the ground. Less than two seconds later, the other two succumbed to Tom's superb marksmanship but by then the sound of gunfire had alerted the whole compound. Tom took off running for cover as men began to pour out of the rusted, rundown structures. He sprinted past the defunct gate and slid behind a row of junked vehicles.

Gangsters were running outside, shouting. Tom watched on his phone as near a dozen individuals running amok outside the installation, frantically looking for the source of the gunfire. All were armed with a motley array of firearms. Ill disciplined, some of the gang members began firing randomly at spots in the surrounding hills.

Taking advantage of the chaos, Tom used his cover and timed his shots to the din of firing weapons as he watched gangsters running and shooting all over the place. Using the bird's-eye-view the drone gave on his phone, he took aim at his targets, and five more gang members fell. Suddenly, a man emerged from a door to the compound and he fired a shot from his pistol in the air and shouted.

"Ceasefire, dammit!"

The gangsters immediately complied.

"Alright, everyone inside," the man commanded. "Now!"

The gang members ran inside the building without complaint. Tom peeked through his cover and reeled back in surprise. Sunglasses. Always chewing. Mustache. It was none other than Detective Nick Hunter. Tom's earpiece came alive again. It was the mysterious digital voice.

"Nicholas Ryan Hunter. Distinguished Service Medal recipient. United States Navy SEAL. Six-year service, dishonorable discharge for grand larceny, and five-year prison sentence as a civilian," the digital voice said.

Great. He was facing a former Navy SEAL, and ex-convict. Ohlgren probably saw his potential and hired him ostensibly as a detective, but in reality, as liaison to the Tridents. *Now what?* Hunter had all the gangsters run back inside. What was his plan? Face him one-on-one? Hunter dropped his gun and lifted his hands in the air.

"Tom Meadows. You can come out now!" Hunter called out. "As per my orders, no one is to harm you. I want you to face me. Just us two. Don't worry, Elizabeth is safe."

Tom's blood began to boil again. *Keep on talking, you bastard*, he thought. As if he could read Tom's mind, Hunter continued.

"We had our eye on you since you've been seeing Lina. You have no idea who you are do you? Do you have any idea who she is? Come and face me and if you win, you and Elizabeth walk out of here alive."

Chapter Ten

Tom knew he couldn't trust that snake, but even if only an ounce of it were true, he was going to take his chances.

Who am I? How do they know Lina? What does she have to do with all this?

A lot of questions circled around in his mind. But the tactical situation would not allow him to place his longing for answers as a priority. Right now, Nick Hunter stood between him and the gang, which had holed up inside, and the gang stood between him and Elizabeth. Tom understood Hunter's method. Should he best and kill Tom he would win even more respect among the Tridents and guarantee a continued working arrangement between the police and them. So, Tom decided he was going to accept this challenge. He dropped his weapons and walked out from his place of cover, his hands halfway up.

Hunter approached, his own hands halfway up. They walked towards each other slowly. Tom, for his part, was cautious. If Hunter was going to pull something out of his sleeve, it'd be around the beginning, so he could gain a combat advantage. Once they were near arm's length from each other they stopped.

"So, you're here to stop us, eh?" Hunter sneered. "If only you knew what I knew you would be kicking your own ass right now."

"I have no idea what you're talking about," Tom replied. "It seems like you know me."

"I do," Hunter replied. "And we thought you died all those years ago. But look who's back from the dead. Now you're here to stop us and I won't let that happen."

"Tell me who I am!" Tom demanded.

"I'll never give you the pleasure!" Hunter growled. "You probably have already pieced together Ohlgren uses the Tridents to traffic girls for money. You're out to stop him, and I'm going to stop you."

"You're one sick and evil son-of-a-bitch, you know that?"

"Gotta pay the bills, my friend," Hunter laughed.

"A lot of people pay their bills without having to resort to vile and evil methods. There are people who would rather starve to death than hurt innocents…"

"You live in an idealistic fantasy world, Tommy boy. A word of advice. In the *very* remote chance you walk out of here alive. Don't nurture that sentimentalist crap. The hard truth of the matter is…it's kill or be killed!"

Hunter brandished a hidden knife and lunged. He didn't know how he was able to do it, but Tom ably and almost effortlessly blocked the attempt to the outside with a sweep of his arm. Then it all came back to him. He remembered. He was trained in the art of Kali-Escrima, a deadly Filipino Martial Art which emphasized both offense and a strong defense, and how to counter with weapons or empty hands. Hunter recovered, however, and was able to slash Tom's right shoulder. Blood oozed from the wound. It was superficial, but painful. Tom winced and grabbed his shoulder. Hunter didn't play fair. *It was supposed to be weaponless...*

No matter. He would need to find a way to disarm his opponent. Tom remembered the rule of thumb when it came to facing a foe with a blade, having nothing. Basically, it was to either run, or find a way to disarm the assailant. Disarming someone who knew what he was doing with a blade was going to be next to impossible. So, he had to even the odds by arming himself.

As Hunter quickly advanced on him, slashing the blade, Tom dodged and ducked, but at the same time was quickly scanning the ground around him. He saw an old, rusted 1-inch pipe that was around two feet in length and determined it would be the perfect weapon for the task. The Marine quickly scooped up the pipe, twirled the weapon around to gain momentum in a classic Escrima move and then brought a ferocious backhanded upper slash aimed at Hunter's weapon hand. Hunter screamed in pain, as his knife flew in the air and landed in a pile of junk, twenty feet away. A bone or two of Hunter's hand might have been broken, as Tom felt the reverberation in his stick.

Enraged, Hunter executed a perfect roundhouse kick that hit Tom's weapon hand, causing him to let go of his own weapon, which went spinning into the ground behind him. Now, it was going to be hand-to-hand.

The combat moves were coming back to Tom's mind, and his muscle memory kicked in, and he knew exactly how to counter Hunter's attacks. Hunter was remarkably strong and quick for a man likely more than ten years his senior. It took Tom all his might to counter Hunter's blows. And he was losing energy. Very soon he knew he would succumb to the agility and superior stamina of the ex-SEAL.

Just when he thought he was going to lose all his strength; Tom heard a buzzing that grew louder. It was the drone! It swooped down and clipped the side of Hunter's head. The ex-SEAL held his hand to his head in pain and looked surprised. Tom knew this was his chance. He lunged forward and spun, landing a hard elbow on Hunter's face, and in his follow through completed a roundhouse kick maneuver that sent a stunned Hunter flying backwards into a pit filled with machinery.

The fall was long, maybe thirty feet, and Hunter landed with a sickening thud on concrete. There was no doubt he was dead. Tom was out of breath and sweat trickled down his face. He walked back to where he had dropped his weapons and retrieved them but holstered the pistols and slung the carbine on his back. He knew he had won their respect, so the Tridents were not going to kill him now.

The main door to the facility swung open, and a large gang member emerged. He said nothing, but merely motioned for Tom to enter and to follow him. Tom complied and was ushered down into a hallway. As he walked, he heard static and his earpiece activated, and the voice spoke to him again. He listened as he followed the large man up flights of stairs into more abandoned hallways until they reached what looked like office doors. Everything seemed to creak as they moved, and the sound of footsteps on metal grating echoed through the entire structure. The doors were opened, and Tom stepped inside.

"Tom Meadows. Welcome," said a slender figure in a suit, seated at a desk. He was probably sixty years of age and was puffing a cigar. He recognized him. It was the man in the pictures with Ohlgren and Murdock!

"I'm Jose Gomez," the man said. "I lead the Tridents. I understand you have information for me?"

Tom nodded. He gave Gomez his phone, who held it up to his ear and listened to the mysterious voice speaking on the other side of the line. After about a minute, Gomez motioned to the gang member who brought Tom there, and he went into another room. A moment he emerged with a confused Elizabeth. She saw Tom and smiled as she ran to him.

"Mister Tom!" she squealed.

Tom knelt and embraced her firmly. A tear fell down his cheek at the thought of almost losing her. He stood and looked at Gomez who gave him an acknowledging nod and motioned to the guard to escort them out.

Moments later they were in the car, headed towards Lina's. The thirty-minute drive seemed like forever, and once they arrived the gate could not open fast enough. Lina was there, tears streaming down her face as Elizabeth ran towards her. Mother and daughter embraced for a long time as they cried together. Enraged at the trauma dealt to the two most important people in his life, Tom had one more thing he needed to do.

He didn't have to utter a word. He looked into Lina's tearful eyes as she embraced Elizabeth. Lina understood, and nodded. She knew what needed to be done, and seconds later Tom was in the car again, driving into Las Cruces proper. This time, he was more deliberate, careful, and calm in his driving. Fifteen minutes later, he had pulled up into the visitor's parking area for the Las Cruces Police Department. He was going to put an end to this. Unarmed, and without his tactical gear, he entered the double doors and straight to the visitor's waiting area where a receptionist at the front desk greeted him.

"Can I help you, sir?" she asked, cheerfully.

"Yes, I need to speak with the Chief of Police," Tom replied. "Tell him Jose Gomez needs to speak with him immediately."

The receptionist did not respond and immediately picked up her phone. She said something into the receiver and listened to what was being told to her from the other line and turned to face Tom.

"You can go on in to see him, sir. Last door in the hallway to your right."

"Thanks."

The receptionist pressed a button and the secured door to the hall was unlocked and Tom could enter. He followed the hallway down to the specified door and knocked.

"Come in!" Chief Ohlgren' voice was heard.

Tom opened the door and entered the office. Ohlgren, seated at his desk, looked confused.

"Wait, you're not Gomez. What's going on here?"

"So, you do know Jose Gomez," Tom said.

"Who are you?" Ohlgren asked.

"That's not important," Tom responded. "What's important is that I know that you, Chief Ohlgren, are trafficking young girls, selling them to the highest bidder. You violated your oath as a law enforcer, and instead abused your position of power to deal in one of the most reprehensible trades in existence. You sick bastard."

Ohlgren laughed incredulously as Tom shoved a picture of him and Gomez leading a blindfolded girl out of a car into his face.

"Oh, come on," Ohlgren smirked. "That's doctored."

Unable to restrain himself, Tom gave the chief a quick, hard punch in the face. Blood trickled from the chief's nose.

"That's assault," the chief growled.

"That's a drop in the bucket compared to what you are going to have to answer for. And that picture? That's also a drop in the bucket of all the evidence we have against you."

"You are in way over your head son," Ohlgren said. "I'm untouchable. You think it's just me? This industry has benefactors in every level of government. You can't touch me. You think the gangs are using us? Ha! We're using the gangs. They profit too much from our arrangement. We're about to cut them out as middlemen and take all their assets. No one will suspect the police as we will just be doing our job in eliminating those thugs."

Tom listened quietly. However, he had been noticing that since the beginning of their conversation the chief had been ever so-slightly sliding his right hand into an area out of view. Perhaps a compartment hiding a gun. But before Ohlgren could make a move, an enormous explosion rocked the station. Shattered glass flew everywhere.

"What the hell—" Ohlgren was on his feet as bursts of gunfire were heard outside. He turned to open a drawer where he kept his service weapon but before he could withdraw it Tom reached over and with one swift move shut the drawer on the chief's hand. Ohlgren yelled and gripped his injured hand in pain. There was more gunfire and voices were heard in the hallway. Moments later Gomez's bodyguard burst through the door. Gomez was right behind him.

"Jose? What the hell is this!?" Ohlgren demanded to know.

Without a word Gomez retrieved a .38 Special revolver from his jacket pocket, aimed it at Ohlgren's head and pulled the trigger. There was a loud report and the chief fell backward into his chair before sliding onto the floor, lifeless. Gomez then nodded at Tom, who nodded back.

Tom took his smartphone out of his front breast pocket and hung up the call. Gomez had been listening in the conversation he had with Ohlgren the whole time; when Ohlgren divulged his intentions on eliminating the gang to Tom, Gomez realized the chief had to be taken out. The Tridents had Rocket Propelled Grenades on the ready, and the attack on the station was swift and efficient.

But now it was time to leave, as law enforcement reinforcements would come in to secure the station soon. Gomez and his bodyguard disappeared into the hallway of smoke, while Tom escaped in the opposite direction, taking advantage of the chaos to elude detection.

::

Several helicopters were seen in the air, heading towards the burning police station in the distance as Tom pulled up into Lina's home. As the gate closed behind him and he exited the car Lina and Elizabeth rushed out to greet him. Tearfully they all embraced.

"It's okay," Tom assured them as they hugged. "It's done. It's over."

Lina shook her head sadly.

"No, it has only begun," she said, placing her head on his shoulder while looking at the smoke on the horizon and at the news choppers flying into the distance.

…To be continued…

Stay tuned for the next novella in the Tom Meadows Series!

SHAKEN FAITH

The Tom Meadows Series

By Jake Victor Guzman

www.brimingstone.press/tommeadows